The Beginning of Prudence

A TEATIME TALES
NOVELETTE

LEENIE BROWN

Leenie B Books
Halifax

ISBNs: 978-1-990607-09-7 (ebook); 978-1-990607-10-3 (paperback)

www.leeniebbooks.com

www.leeniebrown.com

Chapter 1

Thursday, March 4

"Pray, my dear aunt, what is the difference in matrimonial affairs between the mercenary and the prudent motive?"

Fitzwilliam Darcy leaned forward and closer to the far side of his theatre box. So as to not excite the suspicion of his companions, he attempted to make it look as if he was enthralled with the play below. He was almost certain that he knew the voice which had carried from the adjoining box to his.

"Where does discretion end, and avarice begin?" that familiar voice questioned, causing Darcy to wish he could peek around the wall to see if the voice he heard did, indeed, belong to the lady he thought he had escaped by leaving Hertfordshire.

"Last Christmas you were afraid of Mr. Wickham marrying me because it would be imprudent; and now, because he is trying to get a girl with only ten thousand pounds, you want to find out that he is mercenary."

Wickham. Darcy expelled a breath as if he had taken a blow to his abdomen from his sparring partner. It had to be Elizabeth. Who else would have been in company with Wickham at Christmas? He closed his eyes and leaned backward. Had there truly been talk of Wickham's marrying Elizabeth? The thought made Darcy's stomach turn. He stood.

"Where are you going?" His friend Charles Bingley asked when Darcy turned toward the door.

"I need a bit of air."

"Can it not wait a few minutes? The play will not be much longer."

"I will only go to the door and back. My legs could use the exercise." He did not want to stop at the door. He wanted to leave the box and go… where? To the box where Elizabeth was? That would not do. He turned toward the stage when he reached the door.

How was it that Elizabeth was in a box at this theatre? The subscription price for such a seat was not a trifling amount. He should know since he paid that subscription each year.

He went over her words. She had been speaking to her aunt, but was not her uncle in trade? Did he not live near Cheapside and in view of his warehouse? Surely, such a man would not have the funds to purchase a box. Unless, of course, he was one of the wealthy tradesmen that shifted between the realms of lower-class employees and upper-class customers. One eyebrow arched. That seemed to be the best explanation.

Caroline Bingley glanced in his direction for a third time since he had reached the door. This time, she caught his eye and smiled before dipping her head and looking away.

Three months ago, he would have felt the delight of such an action. It was not that he was going to marry her or court her. However, she was handsome, and only a fool would not enjoy the idea of a pretty lady flirting with him. At present, he must be a fool, for he was not enjoying Miss

Bingley's attention, nor had he for some time. In fact, if he were required to give witness at Old Bailey's on the matter, he would have to admit that, since that assembly in Meryton, he found her, and all the other ladies of his acquaintance who batted their eyes and smiled demurely at him, to be downright off-putting.

He shook his head. That was not entirely true. Elizabeth was one of his acquaintances and her smile was not off-putting. Nothing about her was off-putting. However, the idea that Wickham had played court to her enough for talk of marriage to begin was.

"Do you feel less restless now?" Bingley asked when Darcy retook his seat.

"No, but I will remain seated until the play concludes."

He leaned forward. Perhaps he could hear Elizabeth's voice again. He had heard it in his dreams for some months now, and he knew he should not allow himself the pleasure of hearing her in real life, for it would only make his torment greater. Be that as it may, he seemed unable to prevent himself from seeking it. He, apparently, had not been in town long enough to rid himself of his admiration of her. If anything, his heart had grown fonder of her during the separation. It was truly unsettling how much Elizabeth had turned his well-ordered thoughts on end.

"Oh! If that is all."

Elizabeth sounded rather perturbed.

"I have a very poor opinion of young men who live in Derbyshire; and their intimate friends who live in Hertfordshire are not much better. I am sick of them all..."

Darcy leaned back. He was not certain what had prompted Elizabeth's reply, but he was certain he knew of whom she was speaking. Did she truly think so poorly of him and his friends?

He folded his arms and drummed the fingers of his right hand on upper portion of his left arm while he briefly went over his interactions with Elizabeth in Hertfordshire. He was not an overly amiable sort of gentleman, but he had not been too dismissive of her. That could not be the source of her disdain for both him and his friends.

His left eyebrow arched as a thought struck him. Her mind could have been turned against him by Wickham. Indeed, upon rehearsing to himself the conversation he and Elizabeth had had while dancing at Bingley's ball, Darcy was certain the fellow had tried. Still, that did not explain why Elizabeth did not care for Bingley. Bingley had been most welcomed by all the Bennets, including Elizabeth.

Darcy jumped when Bingley poked his shoulder.

"The play is over."

Awareness of his surroundings settled into Darcy's mind.

"So it is," he said.

"It was a good one."

Darcy nodded. "I have seen it before. I only came for you."

"And Caroline," Bingley said with a grin.

"No, just you."

"Are you certain? Caroline seems to think your invitation was for her, and Louisa supports the idea."

"It was not."

Bingley's brow furrowed. "I thought you might be considering her."

Darcy's eyes grew wide. "On what have you based that supposition?"

His friend shrugged. "Just things I have heard Caroline and Louisa talking about."

"They are wrong." So very wrong! Darcy slipped behind Bingley to avoid having to offer Caroline his arm. He had done his duty in escorting her to his box, but now that he knew she thought her chances of snaring him were so high, he had no desire to raise her expectations any more than they were already raised.

"I think I see someone," he lied as he slipped out the door.

"Mr. Darcy?"

It appeared that he had avoided one lady only to throw himself into the path of another.

"Miss Bennet." Darcy executed a stiff bow. Was the whole Bennet family in town? "Miss Elizabeth," he added when he saw her pulling her sister back.

"These are my relations," Miss Bennet said with one of her sweet smiles that faded as quickly as it had appeared. Her complexion paled, and he thought he saw her sway.

"Are you well?" he asked, reaching for her arm.

"No, she is not," Elizabeth replied firmly and a touch harshly, as if Miss Bennet's state of health was his doing.

"I am well," Miss Bennet protested, though weakly. She squared her shoulders and attempted to smile, while her eyes watched something over Darcy's shoulder. He would love to turn to see what it was that had caught her attention, but that would be rude.

"These are my relations, Mr. and Mrs. Gardiner," she continued, motioning to the fashionable couple next to Elizabeth. "Aunt, Uncle, this is Mr. Darcy."

"It is a pleasure to meet you," Mr. Gardiner said.

"You look very much like your father," Mrs. Gardiner said.

"You knew my father?" How would a woman from Cheapside know his father?

"Did not everyone who lived in Lambton?" Mrs. Gardiner's smile was warm and welcoming. She had an open air about her that was unaffected. "I grew up not far from Pemberley."

"You did?" That was shocking.

"I did, and I still have relations that call Lambton home."

Darcy did not know what to do with this information. "I trust they are all well?"

"As far as I know they are."

"We may visit them this summer," her husband said. "Lizzy has agreed to accompany us on a trip to the Lake District, and so, we shall likely spend some time in Lambton if the schedule allows."

Darcy turned his eyes back to Elizabeth. "Have you ever been to the lakes before?"

"No." Her lovely eyes were full of fire. Was that Wickham's doing?

"I hope you enjoy it, and," he turned back to the Gardiners, "I would be pleased if you would visit Pemberley should your time allow. I cannot guarantee I will be home, but the housekeeper gives excellent tours." He hoped he would be home. Perhaps then, he would have a chance to douse that fire of hatred that seemed to flow in waves from Elizabeth.

"Will you be in town long?" he asked her.

"No."

"Lizzy," Mrs. Gardiner scolded softly.

"I am only here until tomorrow," she added. "I am on my way to visit Mrs. Collins."

"Mrs. Collins?" Did Mr. Collins have a wife?

"The former Miss Lucas," she explained.

Once again, Darcy found himself searching for how to reply to such news.

"They could have made the full journey in one day, but then, we would have been sorry to have not seen Elizabeth," Mr. Gardiner said.

Just Elizabeth? Did they not wish to see Miss Bennet as well?

"And Lizzy was desirous to see her sister," Mrs. Gardiner added.

"Have you been in town?" Darcy asked Miss Bennet.

"Did you not know?" Elizabeth's tone was acerbic.

"Why would I?" Darcy retorted.

"Jane called on Miss Bingley, and Miss Bingley called on her." Elizabeth's gaze held his with ferocity.

How long had Miss Bennet been in town? Darcy shook his head. "I knew nothing of either call."

"Did not Mr. Bingley mention it to you?"

"Darcy," the very gentleman who was being discussed said. "I thought you were behind us. It is not like you to…"

Darcy heard his friend's inhale.

"Miss Bennet? Miss Elizabeth?" Bingley stood next to Darcy. "Is this not a delightful thing, Darcy? How long will you be in town?"

"They leave tomorrow," Darcy answered.

"No, *we* do not," Elizabeth retorted. "*I* leave tomorrow. Jane will remain at my aunt and uncle's where she has been for the past two months."

"Two months!" Bingley cried. "And you did not call on us?"

"She did," Darcy replied. "Ask your sisters."

Bingley's eyes were wide with horror. "Miss Bennet called on us?"

"On your sisters."

Bingley took a small step backward as if the words Darcy had spoken had reached out and given him a shove. "Why would they not tell me?"

"You truly did not know?" Miss Bennet, who was being supported by her sister, asked. Tears clung to the lower rim of her eyes. Had he misread her? Did she care for his friend?

"I swear I did not." Bingley's tone was nearly pleading.

This seemingly grave error in judgment on his part needed to be remedied as quickly as could be. He could not and would not knowingly be the source of disappointment for Elizabeth's sister or his friend.

"May we call on you?" Darcy asked Mrs. Gardiner.

"Certainly." The lady looked confused, and her gaze flicked between Jane and Mr. Bingley. "That is, if Jane wishes for it."

"Do you?" Bingley asked.

Miss Bennet nodded.

"Will that not upset Miss Darcy?" Elizabeth asked. Her tone was still fiery.

"What does it have to do with my sister?" Darcy asked in a less than warm tone. "What have you heard about her?"

"This may not be the best place for this discussion," Mr. Gardiner interjected with a glance at the other people milling about in the corridor. "Shall we suffice it to say that Mr. Bingley and Miss Darcy are not on the cusp of betrothal?" The look he gave Bingley was pointed and carried a warning.

"My sister is not even out, and no offer has been present to either her or me by my friend," Darcy answered.

"But it is hoped for," Elizabeth muttered.

"Is it?" Darcy snapped. "I have not heard that it is."

"Miss Bingley said it was."

Darcy closed his eyes. Of course. He shook his head and opened his eyes. If Bingley were not his dearest friend, he would cut Miss Bingley from his acquaintance. "Miss Bingley does not speak for me or my sister," he kept his voice as even and unaffected as he could given the circumstances. "For that matter," he added softy but firmly, "neither does a certain officer in the militia."

"I think it is best if we leave the rest of the particulars until tomorrow," Mr. Gardiner said. "My wife or Jane can write to Elizabeth with the results of our discussion." He made a sweeping motion of his hand toward the stairs at the far end of the hall. "There are children waiting for me at home, and Elizabeth will have an early morning tomorrow."

"May I ask one more thing before you leave?" Darcy waited until Mr. Gardiner gave him permission, then he turned to Elizabeth. "How long will you be in Kent?"

"About six weeks."

He smiled. "That is excellent news, for then, I will be able to answer any questions that remain when I see you there."

"Are you going to Kent?"

"I am. I go every year around Easter to visit my aunt."

"If that is not Providential!" Mrs. Gardiner cried.

Elizabeth cast a withering look of displeasure at her aunt. It seemed she did not agree that her meeting Darcy again in Kent was a gift bestowed by the good Lord above.

"Until tomorrow, Miss Bennet, Mrs. Gardiner," Darcy said with a bow. "Mr. Gardiner," he added with a nod of his head.

Bingley spent a few more words in parting, wishing Elizabeth a good trip and expressing his delight in having seen Miss Bennet and met her relations, while Darcy began to

contemplate how he could improve Elizabeth's opinion of
him.

Chapter 2

Monday, March 23

As the sun started to approach its zenith, Darcy tapped his foot on the floorboards of his travelling coach while he sat in it outside the coaching inn at Bromley.

"Are you well?" Georgiana asked.

"I am anxious to have my journey done." And to see Elizabeth.

During the two weeks since he had last seen her, he had discovered from her aunt and sister a great deal of what she currently understood about him thanks to Wickham's well-twisted version of the truth.

"I am happy you asked me to join you this year."

He took his sister's hand. "I am happy to have you with me."

Indeed, he had been reluctant to be parted from her for many months now. Be that as it may, he had not intended to bring her with him on this trip when he first marked it on his calendar, for he never brought her with him to Rosings.

"Are you certain you are equal to the challenge of our aunt?" he asked. "She can be quite unbearable at times. She will correct and scold even when she has no clue about whatever the topic may be." Lady Catherine imagined herself an expert in all things.

"I know what she is like, Fitzwilliam, and while I will admit to being somewhat anxious, I think I am capable of tolerating her."

He hoped she was.

"Are you prepared for her?" Georgiana asked him. "You know that by bringing me to visit, she might expect that you are finally going to propose to our cousin Anne."

That was a danger. A very real danger. However, it was one which could not be avoided. Wickham had spoken most deceitfully about Georgiana's character to Elizabeth, and in Darcy's mind, there was no better way to prove that Wickham was a liar of the first order than for Elizabeth to meet Georgiana. It would only take a few moments for the two ladies to be in company before Elizabeth would realize that Darcy's sister was the furthest thing in the world from cold.

"You will put yourself properly forward when we meet the new parson's wife and her friend, will you not?" He knew that, at times, his sister could be just as reserved as he was in new situations.

"Of course. If you approve of them, then, so will I."

"In truth, I do not think very highly of the parson," Darcy clarified. "Mr. Collins is a rather pompous and insipid man, who is given to excessive talking. However, his wife, whom I met before she was Mrs. Collins, seemed a sensible sort of lady."

"What about her friend?"

"Whose friend?" Colonel Richard Fitzwilliam asked as he entered the carriage.

"The one who is visiting Lady Catherine's new parson's wife," Georgiana answered.

Richard grinned. "Ah! The reason your brother visited Cheapside so frequently the past two weeks. I must say I am anxious to meet this Miss Elizabeth. I dare say we have never seen your brother so bothered by what some lady might think of him. Would you not agree?"

Darcy scowled as his sister giggled and answered that indeed, she had never seen him so bothered.

"It is not as if I am keeping a secret from either of you, for I have already told all that you need to know about her."

"I know," Georgiana admitted, "but I would like to hear about her again. She sounds lovely."

Darcy sighed. She was lovely. Elizabeth was the loveliest lady he had ever met.

"I will not disagree with you that she is lovely, but I would like you to form your own opinion, and therefore, I will not repeat what I have already shared," he replied. "However, I will ask one favour of you that I have not yet mentioned. I would very much like it if you could help Miss Elizabeth gain a better opinion of me." He cast a wary look at his cousin. Richard knew this part. "I have learned that she has been told some things about me that are only partially true."

"Less than partially," Richard muttered.

"You see..." Darcy looked down at his hand which held his sister's. "She has met Mr. Wickham."

Georgiana sucked in a quick breath.

"He has joined himself to the militia that is stationed near her home. Therefore, Wickham and Miss Elizabeth have been in company often."

"Does Miss Elizabeth... is she...?" Georgiana seemed lost for words, but Darcy suspected he knew what she wanted to know.

"As I have said before, Miss Elizabeth has very little by way of money to add to a marriage, but she is pretty. However, it seems her beauty could not capture him as well as ten thousand pounds could, and as I understand it, he is now paying court to a young lady who has just come into an inheritance of that very amount."

"Oh, dear." His sister's tone was laced with sorrow. She knew intimately how much Wickham favoured money above all else. "Is Miss Elizabeth disappointed? Has he injured her?"

"That I cannot tell you with any degree of certainty." And he wished he could, for it would make him feel much better if he could be assured that the lady who had stolen his heart had not given hers to the likes of Wickham. "All I know is that her aunt seems to think she is somewhat disappointed but not severely injured. I do not know if Wickham has touched Miss Elizabeth's heart or not. She told her aunt that he had not, but her aunt was not entirely convinced."

Richard made a rumbling noise from his side of the carriage that sounded a great deal like a wild beast who was being held back from his supper.

"A discreet word that Mr. Wickham is not to be trusted has been sent from Mr. Gardiner to Mr. Bennet," Darcy assured Richard. "That is all we can do."

"I cannot believe he is so very bad, and yet, I know it is true," Georgiana said.

"I wish it were not true," Darcy assured her. "Miss Elizabeth has already been told about some things pertaining to Mr. Wickham and myself by her sister in a letter, so she cannot now remain completely unaware of his duplicity. You may rest easy though, for no one knows about your involvement with him."

"What are your intentions regarding Miss Elizabeth once Georgiana proves to her that Wickham is a liar?" Richard asked.

"How can I prove that?" Georgiana asked in surprise.

Darcy glared at Richard who had the good grace to look somewhat chagrined. "Wickham did not just deceive her about me."

Panic suffused his sister's features. "What did he say about me?"

"I do not want to cause you pain." Darcy shot another glare in Richard's direction.

"Allow me to do that since I am the one who spoke without thinking." Richard leaned forward and placed both of his hands on Georgiana's knees. "What the blackguard said about you is utterly untrue. He could not have told a greater lie if he had said that snow is the warmest blanket under which someone could sleep. So, when I tell you this, you must know that it has no resemblance to you at all, which is one reason why your brother wants you to meet Miss Elizabeth. Will you promise me that you will not think what he said is true?" He waited until Georgiana gave a small nod of her head. "Wickham said that you are cold and unfeeling."

Georgiana turned wide eyes to Darcy who nodded his agreement.

"Unfortunately," Darcy said, "he was able to base his lie on my behaviour." Oh, that was painful to admit, and the rest was not going to be any easier to share. "I was not very friendly when in Hertfordshire. In fact, I insulted Miss Elizabeth before I had even met her." Miss Bennet had shared that this insult was a part of what had stirred Elizabeth's displeasure with him. It had been the beginning. He regretted his words more than he had been able to express to either Miss Bennet or Mrs. Gardiner.

"You did not!"

"I assure you that I did. I have several sins for which to atone." He looked out the window.

"And once you have gained her favour, instead of her loathing, then what?" Richard asked.

Darcy shook his head and shrugged. "I do not know. I just know I must improve her opinion of me."

"Do you love her?" Georgiana's question was asked softly, almost as if she were afraid to voice it.

Did he love Elizabeth? That was the question of the hour and every hour since before he had left Netherfield, was it not? He nodded slowly. "I may." He scrubbed his face with his hands. "Even though I am not certain it is prudent to do so."

Perhaps this was not the sort of conversation most brothers would have with a younger sister, but his sister had made a very imprudent decision almost a year ago, and he was determined that she would understand what was important in marriage *before* she was presented to society.

"Surely, you cannot fear that she is intent upon snaring you for your money," Richard said. "For it sounds as if she would refuse you if you did offer."

That was true. After seeing the fire in her eyes that night at the theatre, he had no doubt that she would refuse him soundly if he were foolish enough to offer.

"No, I do not fear that. My hesitation is based on the fact that her family has low connections, and her youngest sisters are left unchecked by a silly mother and an indifferent father." He shook his head. "How can I join my family to that?"

"If you marry her, will her family come to live with you at Pemberley?" Richard asked. "Or will it just be Miss Elizabeth? From what you have said about Bingley's fondness for Miss Bennet, I dare say you will be joined to Miss Elizabeth's family whether you deny your heart or not." He leaned back and crossed his arms, looking rather satisfied with his reasoning, while Georgiana popped forward as if struck by a thought that captured her fancy completely.

"What is the term for what Wickham did with me?" Georgiana asked. "You know, the one that describes how he was only pursuing me for my wealth?"

"Greed?" Richard answered.

"No, no, that is not it. Lady Matlock used a term that I am certain began with an *a*."

"Was it, by chance, avarice?" Darcy asked.

"Yes! Just so! Avarice." She smiled broadly. "Avarice is a deplorable thing, is it not?" She looked from Richard to Darcy.

"Most certainly," Darcy agreed, "but I do not see how or why that signifies to this discussion." If someone could just tell him that it was perfectly acceptable to allow himself to consider marrying Elizabeth, that would be useful information. A vocabulary lesson was not helpful.

"It signifies because it seems to me that dismissing a lady just because her purse is not heavy and her family is not as perfect as what one sees in a portrait in a long gallery is very much like avarice, except it is more of its shadow. Therefore, it is not seen as clearly and not thought of as so bad a thing."

His little sister had *not* just compared him to Wickham, had she?

"While it is prudent to marry well, one must not succumb to avarice or its shadow."

He glanced at his sister who pulled herself up straighter and lifted her chin. When in the past year had she become so well-spoken and wise?

"Therefore," Georgiana continued, "I must ask you, Fitzwilliam, about Miss Elizabeth's character? Do you expect her to spend all your money and be a deplorable mother to your children?"

Darcy shook his head. Miss Elizabeth seemed sensible and had, on occasion, seemed quite unhappy with the things her youngest sisters did or said.

"Do you expect her family to bring shame to your name that cannot be repaired?"

Again, Darcy shook his head.

"Will this connection end in your destruction or the destruction of the estate you steward?"

Darcy shared a look of wonder with his cousin. "How do you know to ask all of these things?"

"Mrs. Annesley has told me that I must always begin my evaluation of a gentleman not with his pretty words, well-tailored clothes, or the plumpness of his purse. I am rather to look first at his character."

She sighed as if such an instruction was the most difficult thing she had ever been expected to do. "It is not an easy thing to decipher," she admitted, "but it must be done. Had I known in Ramsgate what I know now, I may have avoided my own disappointment and injury. I saw Wickham treat others with disdain when we were out walking, and I felt the press of his words to do as he said or lose his good opinion. Based on those two things I should have known not to trust him, but he is handsome and charming."

And that was the danger of Wickham. He could talk his way into and out of nearly anything he chose.

"Mrs. Annesley taught you all that?" Richard's tone spoke of how impressed he was with the education Georgiana was receiving under the watchful eyes of her new companion.

Georgiana nodded. "That is only some of what she had taught me. She seems very wise."

Darcy had to agree with that.

She turned to him and took his hands in hers. Her gaze captured his and held it most intently, begging him to listen carefully to what she said. "We must simply evaluate Miss Elizabeth's character before we decide if it is more prudent to make her my sister or to return home disappointed. A little disappointment now is far better than a life of regret, is it not? And is not a little effort of examination now worth more than a hundred thousand pounds?"

Darcy shook his head in wonder. The answer he had hoped to find had indeed been wrapped inside a vocabulary lesson and had been presented to him by a most surprising teacher. "Am I not supposed to be guiding you, instead of you guiding me?"

He looked at Richard. "Ask me again about my intentions."

"Very well. I believe I said something about wanting to know what your plans were once you have improved Miss Elizabeth's opinion of you?"

Darcy smiled as a sense of peace settled over him that he had not felt in many months. "I shall, with the help of you and Georgiana, make a careful evaluation of her character."

"And if her character is not found wanting, which I assume it is not since she has captured your interest and we know you to be excessively fastidious, then what?"

"Then," Darcy said, "I will be free to offer her my heart and seek to win hers."

Georgiana wrapped her arms around his arm and squeezed it tightly as she rested her head against his shoulder. "Oh, I have not been this happy in an age!" She peeked up at him. "Do you think the horses could go faster? I am ever so eager to meet my new sister."

"I have not even convinced her that I am worthy of consideration," he cautioned.

"She will love you," Georgiana assured him. "How could she not? She only needs to know you as we do."

Darcy prayed his sister was correct about that, because he was not sure how to win a lady's heart. He had never actually considered having to do so. He had just assumed that any lady he decided to pursue would accept him with alacrity. After all, he was wealthy and well-connected.

Avarice. He gave his head a small shake. Had he been relying on avarice to find him a wife? Or was it prudence?

What had Elizabeth asked her aunt that night at the theatre? Where does prudence end and avarice begin? Yes, he was almost positive that was it.

He tipped his head so that it rested gently on top of Georgiana's bonnet. The dividing line, he suspected, was found where excellent character, good sense, and ardent admiration met.

Chapter 3

"Good day, Aunt," Richard said as he entered Lady Catherine's favourite sitting room at Rosings. "Darcy, the barouche will be ready for us soon. Perhaps even before your sister is ready since I called for it upon entering my bedchamber." His eyes held a sparkle of amusement, for he, like Darcy, knew that such a statement would not be met with favour by his aunt.

"You have only just arrived," Lady Catherine said. "What can you mean by calling for the barouche?"

Richard gave a look down his nose at their aunt. "There are lands to inspect, my lady, and Father heard you installed a new parson. I am to meet him."

Lady Catherine huffed but did not rise from her chair, though she did lift her feet off her footstool and put them on the floor. "There is no need to go to the parsonage, for Mr. Collins and his wife and cousin are to dine with us tonight, and the lands can be looked at tomorrow. It is not as if they are going anywhere."

"It may rain tomorrow." Richard was excessively good at riling their aunt.

"And it may not."

Richard's lips tipped upwards as if he thoroughly enjoyed the sport of provoking Lady Catherine. His father was the same way when he joined them at Rosings.

"You do not need to take Georgiana with you," Lady Catherine said when Richard ignored her comment about the weather. "She has just completed a long journey. Too much travel is not good for a young lady's constitution."

"In the past, she has travelled further than she did today and survived it," Richard retorted. "Besides, I say that a bit of fresh air in an open carriage is just the thing to blow off the tarnish from hours confined in a closed vehicle. What say you, Darcy?"

"I say Georgiana expressed a wish to accompany us, and I am not willing to deny her the pleasure of a pleasant drive."

"Just because a young lady wishes to do something does not mean that the thing which she wishes to do is prudent." Lady Catherine punctuated what she was saying with a sharp nod of her head.

"I see no harm in it," Darcy answered, "and I say she is going with me."

Lady Catherine's head drew back, and her eyes grew wide, as well they should. Darcy was rarely so direct with her.

"And Anne is joining me," Richard said, drawing both Lady Catherine's attention and ire.

"I should think not! The sun is much too bright."

"The sun cannot possibly touch her in the number of layers you make her wear, but to be as cautious as can be, I will insist she wears her bonnet with the widest brim," Richard replied. "By the by, I have a letter for you from Father. You may read it while we are gone."

This bit of information was new to Darcy. He gave Richard a questioning look, but Richard only smiled like a cat who had just lapped up a bowl of cream and said nothing. The expression was slightly terrifying.

"What does my brother want?" Lady Catherine's tone was filled with suspicion as she took the letter Richard held out to her.

"That you will have to discover while we are out." Richard crossed the room to the door and looked out into the corridor. "Darcy, the ladies are ready."

"Anne is not going!"

"She is, and on this I shall not be moved," Richard said.

"She is not your charge! She is my daughter."

"Read the letter." And with those words, Richard left the room, and Darcy followed.

"What is in that letter?" Darcy asked his cousin as they stood at the bottom of the grand staircase.

"A declaration of independence of sorts," Richard replied with a smile.

The hurried clip-clop of a lady scampering across a room reached them.

"What does he mean Darcy will not be marrying Anne? It has been arranged since they were in their cradles!" Lady Catherine stamped her foot. "I am her mother!"

"And Father is Lord Matlock and head of the family. Your point, Madam?"

"Oh, he is the most infuriating brother in the world!"

"We shall return in an hour or so," Richard said. "I do hope that will give you time to respond to Father's letter with more decorum."

Darcy glanced at Georgiana and Anne. Their expressions were just as surprised as he felt. Richard had always caused a bit of a stir when he arrived at Rosings, but this? Well, this was unprecedented.

Richard offered his arm to Anne. "You are looking in good health today."

"Thank you." She smiled her shy smile. It was a pretty little smile. She was delicate in features and not at all robust in constitution, but there was a graceful beauty to her much like there was in a vase made of the thinnest glass.

"Darcy." Richard tipped his head towards the door.

"I believe you need to tell me what is in that letter," Darcy said as they waited for the carriage to draw to a stop and the steps to be put in place.

"You heard the most important bit of information. Father has declared that you and Anne are not to marry."

Darcy cast a concerned look in Anne's direction. He was delighted by the decree for it meant he would no longer have to come up with polite ways to decline Lady Catherine's suggestions that he and Anne spend time together while he was here.

"I am not disappointed," Anne said as she caught his eye. "And I doubt you are either."

"No, he is not," Richard replied. "In fact, we need you to join us today for a specific reason."

"We do?" Darcy turned his attention away from Anne and towards Richard.

"We do. Father knew you had shown some interest in Miss Elizabeth –"

"Indeed?" Anne cried with excitement. Apparently, she was happier about being free of the possibility of marrying Darcy than the words *not disappointed* might disclose.

"Oh, very much so," Georgiana assured her.

"And how did your father learn of this?" Darcy folded his arms across his chest.

"I told him." Richard held up a hand to indicate that no one should speak until he had finished. "Did you not say that Miss Bennet and her aunt thought you were engaged?"

Darcy nodded. Mrs. Gardiner had been the one to broach that subject during one of his calls in Gracechurch Street.

"That means that Miss Elizabeth also believes it to be true. Therefore, Father has put an end to any possible rumours, and you have gained one more way for Miss Elizabeth to discover that Wickham was lying." He held up one gloved finger as if marking his point. "And *I* have ensured that our source of truth is with us today when we call at the parsonage."

"We are calling at the parsonage?" Anne asked. "I have only driven past a time or two. Mother never let me go in, and she always controls the conversation during dinners, so I have yet to have a good conversation with Mrs. Collins. I think she and I would get on well, but Mother insists it is not for me to befriend one of her station. I suppose it isn't really, but whom else am I to befriend? I will be twenty-five next month, and I have not one particular friend. Not one!"

Richard, who sat next to her, patted her hand. "We will fix that. Father has invited you to Matlock House for the season. A lady your age should have particular friends and even a husband."

Anne sighed. "That would be nice. I have long dreamed of running my own home." She gave Richard a pointed look. "By myself, not with my mother's help."

Darcy chuckled. "I did not know you were anxious to marry."

Anne's eyebrows raised. "Why would I tell you that? If I did, you might actually think you needed to do your duty, and if my mother heard it…" She shook her head but said no more. There was no reason to say more, for everyone in the carriage knew what Lady Catherine would have done.

"Now, tell me how I can help you." Anne pulled herself up as tall as her petite frame could rise. "Shall I lead with an introduction? Miss Elizabeth, this is my cousin whom I have no desire to marry."

"She already knows Darcy," Richard whispered near the edge of Anne's wide brimmed bonnet. "There is no need for an introduction. I suggest we just let the conversation happen naturally. There is no need to direct every interaction, no matter what your mother might say."

"Very well, if you think that is best."

"I do."

"But I do want to help."

"And you will."

Darcy watched the interaction with interest. He could not remember a time when Anne had been as lively as she was today. It would be good for her to be out and away from her mother. He had always suspected that to be true.

"Oh!" Anne leaned out toward the side of the carriage. "I see Mr. Collins is in his garden again. Mrs. Collins encourages him to spend as much time as he likes in it. She says it is good for his constitution and that plants make an excellent audience for practicing sermons."

Georgiana turned to look in the direction Anne was looking. "Is Mr. Collins that man there in the black hat and coat?"

"Yes, that is him. He is very tall and quite broad." She shared a look with Georgiana that spoke of some displeasure. "Of course, it is not exactly the most flattering kind of broadness that a gentleman can have."

Richard chuckled, but Darcy refrained, managing to satisfy his amusement with a smile.

"Miss de Bourgh!" Mr. Collins cried when the barouche approached the low garden fence. He held a small black book in one hand. "I was just remonstrating my flowers on the fruits of the Spirit."

Ah, the notebook must contain a sermon within it.

"And were they attentive?" Colonel Fitzwilliam asked as the carriage stopped.

"Most attentive, most attentive, sir." Mr. Collins bowed low.

"This is my cousin, Colonel Fitzwilliam," Anne said. "And you know my other cousin, Mr. Darcy."

"Oh, yes, yes. We have met. In Hertfordshire. At a ball. It was a fine affair. I am certain that even Lady Catherine would deem it so."

"It must be true if you say so," Anne replied. "I have yet one more cousin with me. This is Miss Darcy."

"It is a pleasure. An absolute pleasure. You do us quite the honour by stopping." He gave the occupants of the carriage another bow. Then, he turned toward the house. "Mrs. Collins, Cousin Elizabeth, come quickly."

"There is no need to hurry them," Richard said. "If you are amenable to it, we thought we would come in for a few minutes. Mr. Darcy has a letter for Miss Elizabeth from her sister."

"You wish to come in?"

Could eyes grow any rounder? Darcy was certain they could not.

"Yes, we do," Anne said with enough authority that surely her mother would have been proud.

"Allow me." Mr. Collins stepped forward and bowed while extending his hand to Anne to help her from the carriage.

"He is interesting," Richard muttered.

"Quite," Darcy agreed.

"Mr. Darcy," Mrs. Collins said as she joined her husband. "Lady Catherine said she was expecting you to arrive, but this is quite the treat to have you call."

"He has a letter from Cousin Jane," her husband explained as the rest of his guests disembarked from their equipage without his assistance. "You do us a great honour by carrying it to Cousin Elizabeth," he said to Darcy. "Does he not, Cousin?"

Elizabeth looked from Mr. Collins to Mr. Darcy. A faint pink stained her cheeks, much like he had seen happen when her youngest sisters were behaving poorly. She knew how to present herself in society, and those of her relations who struggled with that caused her to be uneasy. Darcy could understand that. He was related to Lady Catherine after all.

"I am always happy to receive a letter from Jane, no matter who carries it to me, but I thank you for your service, Mr. Darcy." Her eyes did not quite meet his. That was odd.

"I am happy to be of service." Ah, there. Her eyes finally found his. "May I present my sister and cousin to you?"

She touched her heart, and a question furrowed her brow.

"I brought Georgiana with me specifically to meet you."

Her lovely eyes grew wide at that. "You have?"

"I have. May I present her to you?"

"Of course."

Darcy glanced at Mr. and Mrs. Collins. Mr. Collins looked confused, while his wife wore a somewhat repressed, but excessively smug, smile.

"Miss Elizabeth, this is my sister, Georgiana, and my cousin, Colonel Richard Fitzwilliam. Richard, Georgiana, this is Miss Elizabeth, about whom I have told you."

"It is a pleasure to meet you," Georgiana said as she stepped forward and offered her hand to Elizabeth. "I understand your father owns the estate next to Mr. Bingley's."

"He does."

"And I have heard you dance well, play piano most expressively, and are at least as fond of books as my brother is."

Elizabeth looked from Georgiana to Darcy. "And how did you come to this knowledge? Can your source be trusted? For I am quite certain I do not play piano most expressively."

"Oh, but she does," Darcy replied.

"I noticed that you did not deny dancing well or being fond of reading," Richard teased.

"I could no more deny those things than I could say that the sky is perfectly pink today and was the loveliest shade of purple yesterday."

Georgiana giggled; Richard guffawed; and Mr. Collins looked as if he did not know whether to scold or bow.

"May we come in?" Anne asked.

"Yes, please," Mrs. Collins said. "I will call for some tea. The breeze in the sitting room is lovely today, but if it is too much for you, Miss de Bourgh, please let me know, and I shall close the windows straight away."

"I find today's air quite refreshing," Anne assured her as she led them into the house. "You have done an excellent job making this cottage homely," she effused as she entered the sitting room.

"Miss Elizabeth, I do not want to forget to give you your sister's letter." Darcy's comment allowed for the others to enter the sitting room ahead of him. He took a deep breath. "Before we enter, I wanted to apologize." Georgiana stood just inside the door to the sitting room, waiting for him. "What I said at the assembly was completely and utterly false. I was in a foul temper and was not in a mind to be pleased by anything. It was badly done, and I regret the pain my words have caused you."

Elizabeth stood with the letter he had brought her in her hand, looking for all the world as if she might faint away from shock.

"I pray that you will forgive me. You are both handsome and tempting. I am sorry I did not get the chance to dance with you that night."

Her brow furrowed as she studied him. "I have heard such differing reports of you, and what I have known myself of your character mixed with those accounts has me quite confused. However, I believe I must take you at your word and accept your apology."

It was not an overly warm welcome, but it was far better than the one he had received at the theater.

"That is why I have brought my sister. No one will be better able to tell you the truth of my character than she, and before you say it, no, she will not praise me merely because she is my sister. Neither of us favour disguise, for we have tasted the bitter results of concealment at the hands of a gifted storyteller."

Elizabeth looked down at the letter she held. "You speak of Mr. Wickham."

"I do." Darcy glanced at his sister. "I know my behaviour gave credence to his tales. Please, if you must, think ill of me, but do not think poorly of my sister."

Apparently, that was the thing to say, for it brought a soft smile to Elizabeth's lips and eyes. "I will let her help me form my opinions of both her and you. I will attempt to forget what I have been told, since Jane and my aunt both insist I have been led down a merry path by Mr. Wickham." Her smile faded, and Darcy's heart pinched.

"I am sorry if he has injured you."

"He has injured my pride but not my heart," she assured him.

"Are you certain?" He likely should not have asked that. It was not something he needed to be told, though his heart certainly thought it needed to know the truth of the matter.

One shoulder lifted and lowered. "It would have been an imprudent match."

Wickham had hurt her. "You cannot know how greatly it grieves me to hear he has not left your heart completely untouched."

"Brother?" Georgiana stood at his side. "Mr. Collins is starting to wonder aloud about where you and his cousin are."

"Quickly, tell me if my relations are well and if Mr. Bingley is still calling on Jane," Miss Elizabeth demanded most earnestly. "And then, forgive me for the small bit of disguise I must perpetrate when we enter the sitting room and tell him I was inquiring after my aunt and sister."

"I think I can allow that sort of disguise," Darcy replied with a smile. "Your relations are all in excellent health, Miss Gardiner wished for me to deliver her message of longing to see you soon, and I would say we will be reading an engagement announcement in the papers before long, which will please you, your sister, and your mother, and will make Miss Bingley less than pleased."

"And you?" she asked. "Will you be pleased to have your friend tied to someone like Jane?"

"As I admitted to your aunt and sister, my purpose in separating your sister and Bingley had nothing to do with whether or not she was suitable for him. I truly did not think his admiration was returned in equal measure."

"How could you not see that she adored him?" Miss Elizabeth asked in shock.

"Oh, I can answer that," Georgiana inserted. "My brother can sometimes be quite daft about things, and I have to explain the simplest things about what I am thinking to him."

"I am not daft," Darcy protested.

"Then, tell me; what is Lady Matlock's favourite flower?"

"I do not see how not knowing that is being daft."

Georgiana gave Elizabeth a speaking look. "Our aunt wears a gardenia scented fragrance, has many potted varieties in her house and conservatory, and her favourite brooch is painted with a bouquet of gardenias. I am truly not sure how he could not know that she prefers that flower to all others."

Elizabeth bit back a smile.

"But he is a wonderful brother despite his blindness about some things." Georgiana smiled up at him.

Darcy shook his head. "You see. It is as I told you. She will not praise me just because I am her brother."

"And I am only so forward with you," Georgiana said, "because my brother has said you are trustworthy."

"I appreciate your candor," Elizabeth assured her. "Shall we go in?"

"I think we should," Georgiana agreed.

Darcy stood in the entry for a moment longer enjoying the portrait of felicity that his sister and Elizabeth painted as they chatted while finding a place to sit together, and he knew, without one moment's pause, it was a tableau he wished to be able to witness forever.

Chapter 4

Candles soared on tall candelabras down the center of Rosing's dining table. China, silver, and glass sparkled beneath them. Footmen stood sentry near the sideboards. All was presented to make the best impression of rank and wealth. Lady Catherine was not one to leave a detail to chance in that department.

She and Darcy led her guests into the room. Richard was normally the one who was called upon to escort their aunt to her seat when he and Darcy visited Rosings. However, today, Lady Catherine was seriously put out with him. She had calmed somewhat by the time they had returned from the parsonage, but her displeasure had yet to be appeased.

A season in town with all the presses of people and filth of the streets was not something she wished upon her daughter. Richard had assured her that Anne would not be placed in any untenable situations. Lady Catherine insisted that the whole idea of Anne leaving Rosings was untenable.

The fact that Richard was even being allowed to escort Anne into supper was only due to the fact that their aunt was not happy to allow him to escort Elizabeth while Anne and Georgiana entered together. Darcy had put that idea forward when Lady Catherine was grousing about how that letter had ruined her whole day and the dinner to come.

Therefore, it was Georgiana and Elizabeth who sat down next to each other on Darcy's side of the table.

"That will not do," Lady Catherine said. "Georgiana, you must come up one to be across from Anne. Darcy, you must go down to be across from Fitzwilliam. Mr. Collins switch places with your wife." She smiled when he sat down next to Elizabeth. "That is better. Patterns and forms are important," she explained as she took her seat. "I only am sorry that there is not another gentleman to sit across from you, Mr. Collins."

"Do not fear, my lady. All is well. I can sit wherever you wish and do so happily."

"Yes, I am sure you can." Lady Catherine favoured Richard with a look that said she wished he would be so obliging. That was never going to happen. Richard was rarely obliging when it came to Lady Catherine.

"What a wonderful presentation you have made for us," Mr. Collins continued. "We are so very honoured by your invitation. I am certain my wife and cousin feel it as much as I do myself. I have impressed upon them the privilege."

"Yes, well," Lady Catherine said, "let us not speak about it any further." She looked to the footman at the far end of the sideboard and nodded. Soon, everyone had a bowl of *Spring Soup* in front of them.

"How was your afternoon?" Darcy asked Elizabeth.

"Aside from the lecture about understanding the honour of your visit and my visit here tonight, it was delightful." She spoke softly as she replied.

"I am glad it was mostly pleasant; and your walk to Rosings? Was it good?"

"Aside from the second lecture on understanding the honour of my visit here tonight, yes."

Darcy glanced over her head to where her cousin sat. Why would he feel the need to lecture Elizabeth? Mr. Collins slurped soup off his spoon and looked around as if looking for someone with whom to converse. Darcy swiftly lowered his eyes to Elizabeth.

"Have you walked in the grove since you have arrived?"

She smiled that enchanting smile of hers that always graced her face when she was truly pleased by something. "It is a wonderful place to wander."

"I quite agree. I was planning to walk there with Georgiana tomorrow morning. Would you be favourable to company?"

Elizabeth looked past him to his sister who was answering some question that Lady Catherine had put to her. "She will not mind sharing your attention?"

"Not at all. She is quite taken with you."

"And I must admit that I am quite taken with her. She is not at all what I expected, although I must confess that to me, she seems quiet this evening."

"That is my aunt's doing. She can be overbearing at times, and she has received some news that has not pleased her." To put it gently.

"Oh, I hope it is nothing too serious."

"It is nothing more than confirmation of what has always been, but she has long denied." He lowered his voice further. "I shall tell you about it tomorrow on our walk if that is acceptable."

"Did I not tell you that there is no place so elegant as Rosings, Cousin Elizabeth?" Mr. Collins inserted into the conversation of which he was not a part nor truly welcome to be a part.

"You did indeed," Elizabeth replied.

"And are you enjoying the spectacle?"

"Quite."

"We, my wife and I, dine here once a week."

Was there some significance to the emphasis on the word *wife*? And why did the man look as if he had just delivered a pointed lesson with his words?

"Yes, Charlotte has told me you do, and I am happy for her."

Mr. Collins lifted an eyebrow and seemed less than pleased with the response, though Darcy could not understand why. It was a perfectly formed reply. Thankfully, the man returned his attention to his nearly empty bowl of soup.

At the end of the table, Lady Catherine lowered her spoon and dabbed at her lips. Immediately, footmen appeared to collect bowls. Mr. Collins hurriedly scooped a last spoonful of soup into his mouth.

"Rosings' cook is very good," he said. "Ours is nearly as good. Lady Catherine recommended her to us."

"Yes. I know." Elizabeth answered. "And every meal I have eaten has been delicious. I thank you for your provision."

The man was beginning to grate on Darcy's nerves. Why was he acting as if he were better than Elizabeth? He was heir to her father's estate, but he was not the master yet. At present, he was merely a parson and cousin.

"Tell me, Miss Elizabeth, do you play?" Lady Catherine asked.

"The pianoforte?"

"Yes, what else would I wish to know?"

"I saw a beautiful harp standing near the pianoforte."

Lady Catherine lifted her chin the tiniest bit while a small smile played at her lips. "I do see how you might be confused, but your cousin only mentioned that some of his cousins played the pianoforte."

"Yes, my lady, some of us do, and I am one of them, though to be honest, I do not play as well as I would like." Elizabeth answered politely while the carrot that she was about to eat before Lady Catherine's question hung on her fork.

"Do you practise?"

"Not as I should, my lady."

Lady Catherine's eyes grew wide. "And you admit it?"

"Would you prefer that I lie?"

Richard snorted, drawing Lady Catherine's attention long enough for Elizabeth to eat her carrot.

"A simple yes would not have been a lie. There is no reason to underscore your ineptitude by divulging more information than is necessary." Lady Catherine's head tipped. "Have you had a season?"

"Not in town my lady."

"And why is that?"

"It is because my father cannot abide town, and my eldest sister has not yet married. Therefore, she is the one who gets to participate in a sort of season, while my younger sisters and I must make do with the festivities and gentlemen callers of the country."

Lady Catherine shot a look at Richard. "How interesting. Your father does not enjoy town?"

"No, my lady, he does not."

"Then, how does your sister take part in a season?"

"She visits my mother's brother and his wife, and they escort her to a variety of soirees and entertainments."

"And who is your mother's brother? What is his place?"

"He is a merchant, my lady," Mr. Collins answered.

"A merchant?"

Darcy could tell that his aunt was not impressed by that news.

"A rather wealthy merchant, who is both fashionable and well-spoken," he said in Mr. Gardiner's defense. "I dare say if you met him at a dinner, you would not know he was a tradesman at all. Both he and his wife are very refined."

"And how do you know this?" His aunt's eyes narrowed.

"I have called on them several times these past two weeks when I learned that Miss Bennet was staying with them. I would have called sooner had I known she was in town."

"And who is Miss Bennet to you?" She looked from Darcy to Anne and back.

"She is a friend and the lady whom my friend, Mr. Bingley, is courting."

"Well, as long as you are not. Mr. Bingley would do well to marry above his station."

"Bingley is intent upon purchasing land."

"You have said that before, but he has not yet done it. Perhaps if he marries a gentleman's daughter, he will finally do as he should have already done." She sighed. "But being from trade, he likely does not understand the importance." She smiled at Elizabeth. "I am sure your sister understands the value of land."

"I am sure she does, my lady." She lifted her fork to eat a piece of carrot but then lowered it. "However, she is not mercenary, nor is she the sort to demand things be done to her liking above all else. Not that she is not prudent and does not have things she desires."

Elizabeth seemed to be searching for the correct words to explain her meaning.

"As someone who has met Miss Bennet, I can attest that what you have said is true. She is as genteel as any lady I know, and her gentle serenity surpasses all I have met, save perhaps for my sister." He smiled at Georgiana and then turned back to Elizabeth. "I am looking forward to having her as part of my close circle of friends."

Elizabeth smiled brightly. "There is none so good or beautiful as Jane in my eyes, though your sister does come close."

"That is as it should be," Darcy assured her.

"I hope I get to meet her," Anne inserted.

"I will see that you do," Richard promised her.

"I do not see how you can assure her of anything," Lady Catherine snapped.

"I will be in town with Anne. Did you not read the full letter?"

Lady Catherine arched a brow but said nothing.

"I am to escort Miss de Bourgh to the various activities of her first season in town," Richard explained to the Collinses and Elizabeth, who knew she was to go to town because Anne had happily shared that bit of news at the parsonage.

"Will you go with her?" Mr. Collins asked Lady Catherine.

"I should say I will." She gave Richard a pointed look.

"My aunt is disappointed that Darcy will not be marrying Anne."

"But I am not disappointed," Anne chirped happily.

"Yes, you are," Lady Catherine scolded.

"No, Mother, I am not. I love my cousin dearly, but I do not wish to marry Darcy. We do not suit." And with that, she went back to eating her dinner.

"Are you not engaged to your cousin?" Elizabeth asked Darcy.

"That is what I was going to tell you tomorrow," Darcy whispered as he shook his head.

"But I had heard you were," Mr. Collins said.

"Your source was mistaken."

"I do not see how."

Darcy sighed. "For as long as I can remember, it has been my aunt's desire that Anne and I would marry. My mother, Lady Anne, was her dearest and only sister."

Elizabeth's hand rested on her heart. "I can understand the desire."

"As can I," Darcy admitted. "However, it was never my desire."

"Or mine," Anne inserted quickly with a smile for Richard as if she wanted his approval of her help.

"Never?" Elizabeth repeated.

"Never," Darcy replied softly.

She opened her mouth as if she wished to ask something else.

"I have never wished to marry anyone," he glanced across the table at his cousin, "until recently," he confessed in a whisper.

Chapter 5

"YOU CANNOT MEAN..." ELIZABETH'S eyes were wide as she pointed surreptitiously at herself.

Had he actually just confessed aloud to the fact that he was considering marriage to the lady whom he hoped to make his wife? He was not sure what had possessed him to do so, but he nodded in reply to both her question and his own. "I do."

"Me? You wish to marry me?" She leaned close to him as she asked the question in the softest of whispers.

"I am as startled as you." He pressed his lips together. Had his brain remained in London? Or perhaps it was still lounging in his room upstairs.

Her wide eyes blinked. "Do you consider me against your will?" This time her question was not as soft as the last had been.

"That is not what I mean." Darcy glanced at their dining companions. Richard was watching the exchange carefully. Mrs. Collins seemed amused. Mr. Collins was babbling on about the brilliance of the candles to no one in particular. Anne was smiling as she sipped her wine. Georgiana was studying her plate intently, and Lady Catherine? Darcy dared to look at her.

"What topic are you discussing that has startled Miss Elizabeth so?" One eyebrow arched over a harsh glare.

Darcy looked at Elizabeth. Did he dare to answer honestly?

"He is considering marrying," Anne answered as she placed her goblet on the table. "And I am happy for him and wish him success." Her eyes darted from her mother to Darcy and then Richard. "Have I spoken amiss?" she asked.

"You are not the only one," Richard replied with a pointed look at Darcy. "One does not fire the cannon until one's troops are in place."

"One does if one is not thinking," Darcy replied. "I apologize for the distraction. You may all return to your dinner. However, I do not see why it should be so shocking that I am considering marriage. I am nearly thirty."

"I am not shocked," Anne assured him. "I am just pleased that it is not me whom you are considering."

"Anne," Richard hissed in warning.

"So this is the source of my brother's letter," Lady Catherine said. "You have thrown over my daughter for someone else."

"I have not thrown over Anne. We were never going to marry."

"Exactly," Anne agreed. "I would have said no had he offered." She smiled at Elizabeth.

"I take it that whomever it is that Darcy is considering is someone whom you know, Miss Elizabeth?"

"Yes, my lady."

"And who is this adventurer who has snared my nephew and stolen him from my daughter?"

"He was not stolen from me, Mother. I gladly give him up."

"I was not speaking to you. You will remain silent until I am," Lady Catherine snapped.

Anne gasped and rose from her place. "No, I will not remain silent. This is precisely why I would never have accepted Darcy. He is handsome to be sure, and he is wealthy as wealthy can be. I adore his sister, and I would relish the thought of living so far removed from you. But *he* is too easily swayed by your temper, Mother. He likes peace. Craves it even." She favoured Darcy with one of her sweet, small smiles. "And had I loved him in such a way that I wanted to marry him – which I never have and do not," she said this part to Elizabeth, "I would have feared your interference in my life forever, Mother, and that I will not countenance." She picked up her wine goblet and looked at a footman who quickly came to fill her glass with wine. She gave him a nod. "I think I would like to take my dessert in the sitting room."

"You will sit down and eat where it is proper to eat."

"No, I will not, Mother."

"Anne, please," Richard said. "Are you truly going to leave me?"

"You wish for me to stay?'

He gave one nod of his head, and Anne took her seat.

"I am not staying because you said to, Mother."

"I do not know what has possessed you to behave and speak in such a manner."

Darcy had to agree with his aunt on that. Anne was behaving very out of character from how she normally was. Not that he found her behaviour to be abhorrent. Indeed, it was rather pleasant to see her finding her voice.

"You, Mother. You are the source, and Uncle's letter is the spark, for I no longer fear being forced to marry where

I do not want to marry." She looked at Darcy. "I do love you, but..." She shook her head.

"I completely understand. The feeling is mutual."

"One does not marry for love," Lady Catherine said. "One marries because it is the right and proper thing to do."

"Some marry for love," Darcy countered. "Father loved Mother, and she loved him."

"Lady Anne was blessed. How could anyone not love her?" His aunt wore a wistful expression.

"I am not sure it would be possible," Darcy admitted.

Lady Catherine shook her head. "I must speak with my brother."

"It will not change things." Darcy took a sip of his wine before continuing. "My heart belongs to another, though she does not know it." He took another sip of wine. This one also did nothing to calm the galloping of his heart. "Indeed, I doubt she would accept me if I offered." A smile tipped the right side of his mouth. "She sees me for who I am – a flawed and sometimes disagreeable man. She knows of my wealth, or part of it, and yet, she would still turn me away. I have not hidden my connections to you or my uncle. Many would overlook the most grievous of insults to secure such ties." He shook his head. "But not her."

Lady Catherine's brow was furrowed. "Is she deficient in intelligence?"

Darcy chuckled. His heart rate began to calm somewhat. "Not at all. She has a quick, keen mind. She just knows what she is worth."

"Is she an heiress?" Lady Catherine still looked confused. "Anne is an heiress."

"No, she is not an heiress."

"Then, I do not see how her worth signifies."

"As my sister has so wisely told me, just today, as we were travelling from London, it is a person's character that is of greatest significance when contemplating marriage. The lady who has unwittingly captured my heart is worth more than any fortune that could be amassed. She is noble in character if not in standing. She loves fiercely. I have seen it in her care for her relations. She values excellence in character above worldly possessions – as she should. She is forgiving, even when she is not certain she wishes to be." He dared to cut a look in Elizabeth's direction as he pretended to take in his whole audience with a glance. She looked shocked but not angry. He decided to take that as a good thing.

"She sounds like a paragon of perfection," Mrs. Collins said with a flick of her eyebrows when Darcy looked in her direction.

"No, she is not that. None of us are, and just like the rest of us, she has her flaws."

"Is she pretty?" Mrs. Collins's lips twitched as if she wanted to smile.

"Bewitchingly so, with the most enchantingly expressive eyes."

"Then, what, pray tell, keeps you from offering for her?" Mrs. Collins's eyes fairly danced with amusement. She knew of whom he spoke. He was certain of it.

"As I said, if I were to offer, she would refuse. To this point in our acquaintance, I have not been the man she deserves."

Mrs. Collins did smile at that. "Had she heard your description of her just now, I am not so certain she could continue to think that."

"Oh, indeed," her husband inserted. "It was a very passionate recital of her qualities. Is his description apt,

Cousin Elizabeth? Not that I doubt Mr. Darcy, of course."

Elizabeth shifted her gaze from Darcy to her cousin. "I am certain that I could not say, for I have never viewed her through Mr. Darcy's eyes."

"Until now," Mrs. Collins inserted.

"Yes, until now," Elizabeth agreed.

"I still cannot approve of the match," Lady Catherine said.

"My father can and does," Richard inserted.

"You know who she is?" Lady Catherine asked.

Richard nodded. "We have met once or twice."

"Is she as Mr. Darcy described?" Mr. Collins asked.

"I have learned to never doubt my cousin's evaluation of a person's character. He is rarely wrong. Occasionally, he might be deceived, but in this instance, from what I have seen, he is not."

"Our food grows cold," Darcy said. "Should I ever be fortunate enough to secure the lady whom I have described, it will be my pleasure to introduce you at some future date."

"I still cannot approve," Lady Catherine insisted.

"That matters not," Darcy retorted before turning his attention to what remained of his meal. He was not certain he could eat it, but he had to attempt to turn the attention away from him and Elizabeth in some fashion.

"You must play for us, Miss Elizabeth," Lady Catherine decreed. "Georgiana can play after you do." She waved one of the footmen to her side. "See that tea and dessert are set up in the drawing room with the piano."

"I thought it was improper to eat in there," Richard taunted.

"It is when it is not part of the plan. Now, it is part of the plan, so, therefore, it is acceptable."

"Will you still allow my sister and I to walk with you tomorrow?" Darcy asked Elizabeth. "I would understand if you did not wish for it. I know I have startled you with my confession. I had not meant to say anything, but..."

"But, what, Mr. Darcy?"

"I do not know other than to say I spoke without thinking. I apologize. It was poorly done." He watched her as she cut a tiny piece of pork and prepared to put it in her mouth.

"Was it true?"

"Every word of it, and it still surprises me that it is, for I have only just come to realize everything my heart has been trying to tell me."

"Why are you whispering?" Lady Catherine asked.

"We were just discussing the lady of my heart."

"I would prefer you did not." She scowled at Darcy. "Not while my daughter, whom you have shunned, is present."

"I have not been shunned, Mother."

"You have if I say you have."

"Mother, I love Richard. I always have."

"You what?" Lady Catherine sputtered.

"I love Richard."

Darcy looked at Richard who merely shrugged and continued eating.

"Are there any other secrets?" Lady Catherine demanded as she placed her utensils on her plate and rose, indicating that their meal was over.

"None of which you need to be aware," Richard answered. "Anne has only ever had me and Darcy from whom to choose. If she still finds she prefers me at the end of her season, then, we will marry."

"How can you do that?" Georgiana asked.

"Do what?" Richard replied.

"Do you love Anne?"

Richard nodded.

"Then, how can you allow her to choose someone other than you?"

Richard rose from his place and offered his arm to Anne. "I would rather have a little disappointment now than have her live with a lifetime of regret."

"A little disappointment?" Georgiana scoffed. "You cannot love her very much if that is all it would be."

"Very well," Richard said. "I would rather sustain a mortal wound than suffer a lingering, though just as deadly, injury by having to live with a wife who regrets her choice."

Georgiana smiled. "That is better. I was worried for a bit that our cousin might be in love with an unfeeling cad."

"Unfeeling cad?" Richard repeated. "I will have you know that I am not a cad. A cad would not care if Anne's heart were injured because of lack of experiencing life."

"You are right, of course," Georgiana said.

"I am indeed," Richard agreed. "A cad," he muttered as he shook his head.

Darcy waited until Georgiana had linked arms with Elizabeth to go to the drawing room, then, he offered his arm to his aunt.

"Are you well?" he asked. She had been quiet for some minutes. She had not even scolded Georgiana for speaking so freely, as he had expected her to do.

She shook her head. "It is not how I thought it would be."

"Perhaps not. But I do believe it is how it is supposed to be."

"How could you not love Anne?"

"It is not that I do not love her. It is just not the sort of love that inspires marriage." He covered her hand which lay on his forearm with his free hand. "I know you are disappointed, but do you not want your daughter to be just as happy as my mother was?"

"She was supposed to be happy with you." Tears filled his aunt's eyes. In all his life, Darcy had never seen her close to tears.

"But she would not have been, and that would have been an even more painful thing for you and me to bear. I know what your wishes have been for us, and I have not said anything so set against those wishes until now because I knew you would be disappointed and angry. I hope that one day you can forgive me and Anne for this momentary sorrow."

"The goal of my life as her mother being dashed, as it has been, is more than a momentary sorrow."

Darcy sighed. Reasonable was not a word often associated with his aunt. "Compared to a lifetime of unhappiness for me and Anne, it is."

"But your mother…"

"She would not want either Anne or me to be unhappily matched." He knew his aunt would never argue that her sister was anything other than the most loving and caring person to have ever lived.

"I still do not like it."

"Nor do you have to. However, that does not change things." He led her to her favourite chair, next to which a table had been laid out with tea and tarts. "I only hope that one day, you can be happy for Anne, and maybe even for me."

She pursed her lips and was silent for a moment before saying, "Maybe one day."

To Darcy's mind, that was as good as a blessing, for rarely did Lady Catherine show any hint of bending from her position on something. Perhaps miracles were possible, and if they were, perhaps tomorrow's walk would prove to be better than expected and the delightful prospect of his sister's and Elizabeth's heads bent over music at the pianoforte, as they were now, would become a regular part of his future.

Chapter 6

TUESDAY, MARCH 24

MORNING DID NOT COME quickly enough for Darcy. The night had seemed to drag on and on, but then, when one was not sleeping, they often felt as if they passed at the pace of a child on his way to a lesson he did not want to do. He had dozed between moments of wakefulness; however, he had been too anxious to do more than that.

At the end of the evening, Elizabeth had still been willing to meet with him this morning. She had even told him where she planned to take her morning walk and at what time.

He looked at his watch again. That time had passed two minutes ago.

"She will be here," Richard said. "I am certain it cannot be easy to get away from the parsonage if one encounters the loquacious Mr. Collins in the process."

Or she might have reconsidered, and he'd find a message from her when he returned to Rosings.

"Any number of other things may have also detained her," Georgiana added. "Perhaps we should walk in the direction of the parsonage to meet her."

"That is an excellent idea." Walking was much better than just standing. Movement dispelled nervousness. Being idle allowed those bothersome nerves to congregate and cause all sort of disagreeable symptoms, like the faster than normal beating of his heart.

"Will you ask her to marry you properly today?" Georgiana had been quite delighted by Darcy's inadvertent broaching of the subject at dinner.

"I had thought to call on her for two weeks before even raising the topic at all. However, since I waited barely more than one call and a few hours, I suppose I must address the subject now. That being said, I am not certain she is willing to answer a request yet. She barely knows me, after all. What idiot implies he is going to offer for a lady when he has only just begun to attempt to win her good opinion?"

"An utterly besotted one," Richard said with a chuckle. "I dare say, Georgiana, that we have never seen your brother act so rashly as he has since arriving at Rosings."

"I think it is sweet, and I hope that when I find a gentleman to love me and describe me as wonderfully as Fitzwilliam did Miss Elizabeth, he will be just as turned about and anxious to declare himself to me." She sighed wistfully. "It was very romantic."

Despite his chagrin to have inspired such fanciful notions in his sister's mind, Darcy gave her an appreciative smile. At least, she had not poked fun at him for making a cake of himself. Of course, he was not about to let her comments pass without some attempt at bringing them back to less-fanciful footings. Therefore, he said, "I hope whoever proves to be good enough to secure your hand is a bit more in possession of his mind than I seemed to be yesterday."

"I hope he is not," his sister insisted.

"If he wishes for me to approve of his suit, he might wish to be," Darcy grumbled.

"If he wishes for *me* to approve of his suit, he best be enamoured so much that his heart bubbles forth with all that is in it," Georgiana retorted. "I want to know his heart completely. I do not want anything left to assumption. I have had my fill of pretty words with no meaning. A gentleman who is normally staid and steady but who seems to forget himself when speaking of his hope for a happy future together with me would be my preference."

He could allow that reasoning, and he conveyed his approval by covering her hand on his arm with his own and giving it a gentle squeeze. "I will not approve of anyone who cannot demonstrate to me that he cares for you more than he cares for anything else in the world. However, I do think he might be able to do that without blurting his intentions during a meal."

Georgiana giggled. "I must say I was glad Aunt Catherine did not hear you."

"I was glad for that and for Mr. Collins not hearing me either." It was likely the first time since meeting that particular gentleman that Darcy had found himself appreciating the man's propensity to excessive verbosity.

"He does seem to be a less than observant sort of fellow," Richard said.

"Thank the Lord he is," Darcy replied.

"Do you think he will pose an issue for you?" Georgiana asked.

"No, for I do not intend to ask him for permission to speak to his cousin. I have written a letter to Mr. Bennet, and I have only to receive Miss Elizabeth's permission to send it to him." He stifled a yawn.

"That is why you seem tired. Were you up all night writing that letter?" Georgiana asked.

"No, but I did not write just one letter."

"To whom else did you write?"

"Elizabeth," he replied softly. "I had to get all my words out on paper so that perhaps today, my mind could be well-ordered." He feared that no amount of preparation could keep his thoughts in tidy lines when he was with her. She truly did set him at sixes and sevens. Surely, this feeling of being set adrift without a sail or oar would cease as soon as he had secured her hand, would it not?

"Well," Richard said, "it appears that we are about to discover if your preparatory work was time well-spent or not."

A bonnet could just be seen over a row of tall bushes near the start of the lane in which they walked. Moments later, a snorting and huffing sow entered the path in front of them.

"Stop her!" Elizabeth shouted to them as she hurried into the lane. "Betsy! Stop."

"Betsy?" Richard muttered before moving to the right side of the path and leaving the left for Darcy and Georgiana. "Come here, girl," he called to the pig. He squatted down and held his arms wide as if welcoming a child to run to him.

Betsy stopped and looked at him.

"Stay here," Darcy whispered to his sister. Then, slowly, he crept towards the sow.

Elizabeth had also slowed her pace and was moving cautiously toward the pig.

"That is an excellent girl, Betsy. Shall we take a walk together?" Richard continued to chat to the animal.

Betsy snorted, and Darcy swore her head bobbed up and down as if agreeing to take a walk with his cousin. He pressed his lips together to keep from laughing.

"Come now, Betsy. Join me." Richard waved for the pig to come to him, and if Darcy had not been there to see it, he would have never believed that the animal obeyed.

As it was, the activity shocked him so much that he stood still and watched.

"Perhaps we can find an apple for you," Richard said.

Again, the sow snorted and seemed to nod her agreement.

"Maybe we can find a pretty bow for your neck," Richard added.

This got a huff in reply, but the sow was now within Richard's reach. He stroked her nose and then her head as she came closer. Finally, he wrapped his arms around her neck. "Do either of you ladies have a ribbon we could use?

Elizabeth untied the ribbon from her dress.

"Miss Elizabeth is going to help you dress, my lady," Richard said to Betsy, who seemed content to be petted by him.

Elizabeth carefully wrapped the ribbon around Betsy's neck and tied it in a knot. "You will need to cut this to get it off her," she said softly to Richard. "But I would rather sacrifice a bit of ribbon than spend another half hour trying to catch her."

"Do you hear that, Betsy? Miss Elizabeth thinks you look fetching in your new blue ribbon. I dare say all the other pigs will be jealous."

"That is not exactly what I said," Elizabeth replied with a laugh, "but if that is what works, you may tell her that she is the prettiest pig that ever strolled the groves at Rosings."

Richard gave Betsy's head a rub. "That she is, for I have never seen another pig walking here before." He rose and took the ribbon in his hand. "Come along, my dear, we must walk you back towards your home so that the gossips cannot tarnish your name too greatly."

Betsy huffed and snorted, but then, she began walking next to Richard as if it were quite the natural thing for her to be led around on a ribbon.

"I cannot say I have ever seen anything like that," Georgiana said as she joined Darcy and Elizabeth.

"Neither have I," Darcy agreed.

"If you are talking about someone speaking to a pig as if they were a person, then, I would have to say I have seen it before. If you are talking about a pig wearing a ribbon and being led around, well, I would have to admit to having seen that as well," Elizabeth said as she placed her hand on Darcy's proffered arm.

"You have?" Georgiana cried.

"I have. My youngest sister Lydia was enamoured with Longbourn's pigs when she was little. I think she still prefers them to most of the other farm animals."

"Why pigs?" Darcy could not fathom what endeared a pig to a child.

"They did not peck like the chickens, were not so large as the donkeys, horse, and cows, and did not have sharp claws like kittens."

Darcy's brow furrowed. "I suppose that makes sense."

"Did your sister talk to the pigs?" Georgiana asked.

"She still does," Elizabeth replied, "though she has given up trying to dress them and rarely walks them on a ribbon any longer."

"Your sister, Miss Lydia, used to play with the pigs?" Darcy was having a difficult time reconciling the Miss Lydia he knew with the image that Elizabeth had just painted of her.

"She did, and she still will not eat a morsel of pork of any sort."

"Pigs," Darcy said in amazement. "I truly would not have thought Miss Lydia fond of any animals, save for maybe a kitten."

Elizabeth laughed. "It does seem odd. She is all fashion and fuss about everything, except pigs."

"How old is your sister?" Georgiana asked.

"She is not yet sixteen. She is the youngest of all of us."

"Then, she is my age. Well, nearly. I am already sixteen."

"You seem much older than my sister. She is not so sensible as you," Elizabeth said.

"Oh, I have only just learned to be sensible." Georgiana caught Darcy's eye and held his gaze. "I was nearly ruined because I, very nonsensically, listened to the charming words of a handsome gentleman who was only interested in my money and not my heart."

Elizabeth gasped. "Surely not! And he said you were... How could he?" Her tone was one of hurt mixed with anger. "Was my aunt correct, then? Is Mr. Wickham a fortune hunter?"

"You know about him and me?" Georgiana's voice did not sound as panicked as Darcy expected it to.

Elizabeth stopped walking. "I did not until you said what you said." She looked anxiously from Georgiana to Darcy. "I would never share what I know with anyone. Ever."

"I know," Georgiana said.

"You do?" Both Darcy and Elizabeth asked in unison.

Georgiana nodded. "My brother told me how you cared for your sister Jane and how upset you were to discover that he had been part of keeping her and Mr. Bingley apart. A lady who cares that deeply for her sister would not share my secret." She gave Darcy a sly smile. "Especially, if my brother can convince you to be my sister." She removed her hand from Darcy's arm while he tried to catch his breath. "I think I should go meet Betsy."

Darcy blew out a breath. "That was not how I had hoped to approach what I said last night, but…" He looked at Elizabeth. "If you are willing to discuss it, then…" Yes, all that preparation in place of sleeping had done him absolutely no good at all now that she was here, next to him, in person.

He shook his head. "I wrote a letter to your father and one to you as well." He pulled both folded pieces of paper from his pocket. "I wanted to be prepared in case you were agreeable to my petitioning your father for your hand."

"You wrote me a letter?"

His eyes met hers, and he nodded.

"Why?"

"Because I was afraid that I would bungle what I wanted to say, which I have." A gentleman of his intelligence should be able to present himself to a lady without fumbling.

"What did you write?"

He looked at the envelopes he held. "That I love you and think I always shall. I missed you greatly while I was in town, and I have come to realize all too clearly since arriving in Kent that I cannot imagine a happy future for myself if you are not in it." He shrugged. "You are, in every way, the very lady who is best suited to me, and the only one who has captured my heart."

"Is that all that you wrote? It is beautiful, but is there nothing more?"

Darcy lifted his eyes to hers, which shimmered with unshed tears. "Yes, that is the extent of it. I am pleased you like it." She did like it, did she not? She had said it was beautiful, but she was also on the verge of tears. Were they tears of delight? He surely hoped so.

"Did you ask me anything in your letter?" Her smile held a touch of amusement.

He blinked and shook his head. How had he forgotten that part? Was it not the whole purpose of all the other confessions? "Forgive me. You are correct. I did ask you something in my letter. I asked if you would consider accepting me as your husband."

"We barely know each other."

"I know that, but –" He stopped talking when she shook her head.

"However, what I know of you now recommends you to me highly. Your sister," she glanced in Georgiana's direction, "proves what I was beginning to suspect from my sister's and aunt's letters concerning you. You are among the best of men." She held her hand out to him, and he took it. "It would seem to rather be in poor taste to refuse such a man, do you not think?"

Hope bubbled up inside Darcy. "Does that mean you are accepting my offer? Will you marry me?"

She brushed at a tear that escaped her eye. "Some would say it is imprudent to marry a man on such short acquaintance, and some would say it is the height of foolishness to believe myself in love with him based on a few letters and a pretty declaration of my value at a dinner party."

"But what do you say?" He took a step closer to her.

"I say that I do not care if I am thought of as foolish, and I do not wish to be prudent."

He stuffed his letters back in his pocket and cupped her cheek with his right hand. "Do you know what I would say?"

She shook her head.

"I would say that to deny one's heart without an excessively compelling reason and to refuse to do what could be done today because someone else thinks it is best done next month is the height of foolishness. However, to claim one's love and to believe in the possibility of a lifetime of happy todays and tomorrows is just the beginning of prudence."

His other hand cupped her left cheek so that her face was framed by both of his hands. "Will you have me? Shall I send my letter to your father?"

"Will you give me the one you wrote to me?"

He nodded. Why could she not just answer him already? His heart was about to gallop away without him. "If you are going to refuse me, do it quickly. I am a dying man as it is."

"I could never refuse you, not now that I know you." She tucked her bottom lip between her teeth as her eyes fell to his mouth.

"I am taking that as a yes," Darcy told her as he lowered his lips to hers.

Her arms wrapped around him, pulling him to her. One of his hands moved to the back of her head while the other encircled her waist and brought them even closer together. Somewhere in the background, Darcy could hear a "Cousin Elizabeth," being said rather frantically, but he was in no mood to humour Mr. Collins by allowing Elizabeth to do anything with her lips but kiss him. Happy and disgruntled relations could wait, for if he was going to begin being prudent by kissing Elizabeth, he was going to do as he had always done things – most thoroughly.

Chapter 7

SATURDAY, APRIL 11

DARCY STOOD AT THE window in Lady Catherine's favourite drawing room. Outside, on the drive, stood his travelling coach. Behind it, was a secondary equipage for his servants and luggage. They had already called at the parsonage to retrieve Elizabeth's things.

"I wish I were going with you," Anne said as she came to stand next to him.

"It is not many months until your season begins. This one has almost concluded, and soon the people you would wish to see will be headed to their country estates."

Anne sighed.

"Do not tell anyone," Darcy whispered, "but Richard plans to speak to his father about your attending my wedding and then, going to Matlock for a few weeks this summer."

His cousin gasped. "Oh, how delightful!"

"What is delightful?" Lady Catherine asked.

"Nothing." Anne pressed her lips together.

"I do not like secrets." This was said with a glare for Darcy.

There had been an abundance of displeasure to be endured from his aunt when she discovered that he had been seen kissing Elizabeth in the grove on that happy day nearly three weeks ago when she had accepted his offer.

"It is time for our walk before I leave," Richard said as he came into the drawing room.

It was customary for Anne and Richard to take a stroll through the close garden before Richard joined Darcy in his carriage. It was only this year that Darcy understood the activity was more than just two cousins getting some air before one would be cooped up in a carriage and the other would be relegated to the confinement of Rosings and her mother.

Darcy watched Anne take Richard's arm. She was wearing that small smile of hers again.

"She is quite beautiful when she smiles," he said to his aunt as he leaned against the window frame. "She rarely smiles at me like that. She looks perfectly happy, does she not?"

Lady Catherine joined him at the window. "She does," she admitted.

"And does it not make your heart glad to see her so?"

His aunt heaved a great sigh. "You will not desist with your questions until I agree, will you?"

Darcy chuckled. "No." He had been pointing out Anne's happiness at every turn to his aunt for nearly three weeks now. "But I would hope you are agreeing because it is true and not because you wish to be rid of me."

One eyebrow arched over a stern glare. "I do not wish to admit the truth. It is not what I wanted."

"But it is what is best for everyone."

Lady Catherine huffed. "I do not see how it is best for me. He will take her from me and not let me see her as often as you would."

"And you are going to allow that?" Darcy knew better than to think his aunt would play the victim and remain at Rosings when she wanted to see her daughter.

Lady Catherine shrugged, while a small smile played at her lips. Though Richard was, surprisingly, retiring from his position in His Majesty's forces, he was likely to find the greatest and most challenging battle of his life lay before him.

"Do try to let her enjoy her life," Darcy cautioned. He would not plead with his aunt to spare Richard from her machinations, for he knew Richard would enjoy his life much more if he had an opponent against whom to match wits. They would be good for each other. "You know my mother used to look at my father the same way Anne looks at Richard."

Lady Catherine pressed her lips together and nodded. "I remember. That smile was as bittersweet then as it is now, for it separated me from my sister, and now it will separate me from my daughter."

"Life changes," Darcy said as his sister entered the room. "My turn to taste the bittersweetness of separation is coming soon." It was only a year until his sister would be presented to society. "Trust me when I say I understand somewhat of what you feel."

"You will have your wife to help you weather it." His aunt's voice was gentle. "I have no one."

"You could have someone. There is no reason that you could not join your daughter for the season and find a husband."

A broad smile spread across his aunt's face. "That could be entertaining, and it might just cause my brother a bit of grief that he well-deserves. My duties to Anne are done now that he has ordered her away to London."

Darcy shook his head. He wished both Richard and his uncle well. Their upcoming season was going to be one neither of them would forget.

"And," Lady Catherine continued, "I will be able to assist your wife as she makes her debut amongst the *ton*." She chuckled as Darcy sighed. "Yes, you are correct, perhaps this is how things should be. I may even be free to help Georgiana when it is her turn."

"No. She will have her new sister for that, and I will abide no interference between them."

"I may test your resolve. After all, you did throw over my daughter to marry beneath you."

Darcy would have taken that comment as a grave insult had it not been accompanied by one of his aunt's rare, taunting looks.

"Challenge me if you must, but I dare say you will not succeed." He pushed off from his place of repose. Elizabeth was just entering the walk that led to Rosings' front door. "Come, Georgiana, Elizabeth is here."

Lady Catherine leaned forward to peer out the window. "You allowed her to walk? What kind of a gentleman are you?" She scampered after Darcy. "The proper thing would have been to call at the parsonage for her."

"She wished to walk. It is one of her favourite pastimes. How could I deny her that?" Darcy replied.

"I still say it is not proper, and I am still not certain I approve of the match."

"Whether you approve or not, the match is made, and very happily so. I do hope you can one day be happy for me."

"Maybe one day," his aunt muttered, and he knew that she was not as disgruntled as she tried to make everyone believe. There was a heart of something other than ice that beat in her chest. She loved her daughter, and she loved her niece and nephews – yes, even Richard, though she would likely protest that fact the loudest and longest.

"Lady Catherine." Elizabeth greeted Darcy's aunt with a curtsey and a smile. "I am delighted to see you before we leave. I have written my thanks to you in this letter, but I am so much happier to be able to offer it in person."

His Elizabeth had surprised him. He had known she was not the sort of lady to faint away or be intimidated by much, but the way she had risen to the challenge of his aunt's less than welcoming ways had been a revelation of just how resilient she was. She had also borne up well under her cousin's lectures in the grove on the day when she had made Darcy the most fortunate man in the world by promising to be his.

"That is very kind and proper of you," his aunt replied.

"I hope you do not think me too forward, but I wished to give you a small token of my gratitude in having allowed me to spend so much time with your daughter and in your home." She took a small parcel from her reticule. "There is a vase on the table next to the pianoforte that seemed to be wanting a small bit of prettiness on which to stand."

His aunt untied the bundle she had been given to reveal a small, embroidered, round piece of cloth.

"The stitches are not as neat as they could be, but if you do not show anyone the back, then, only you and I will know." She smiled at Lady Catherine, who gave her a stern look.

"One does not point out one's ineptitude," Darcy's aunt scolded as she turned the cloth over. "I would have known of it as soon as I looked," she added.

"Which is why it seemed foolish to deny it," Elizabeth replied. "I hope you like yellow roses."

Lady Catherine smiled. "They are my favourite."

"I suspected they might be," Elizabeth said at the same time that Darcy said, "They are?"

"Yes, they always have been." His aunt was looking at him as if it was something he should have known. "A large portion of my rose garden is given to yellow roses, and the vase Miss Elizabeth mentioned is painted with them."

"I never noticed."

This reply earned Darcy a cluck of his aunt's tongue and a shake of her head.

"I do not wish to speak poorly of your nephew and my betrothed, but I hear he can be a bit daft about such things," Elizabeth whispered to Lady Catherine. "Georgiana told me that he did not know that Lady Matlock's favourite flower was a gardenia."

"Indeed?" Darcy's aunt cried. "However did he not know that?"

"I do not see how I am supposed to know these things without being told," Darcy grumbled.

"I did not have to tell Miss Elizabeth which flower I preferred." His aunt looked him up and down. "I may have to approve of this match after all, for it seems you need someone with a keen, observant mind."

"I thank you for the compliment, my lady."

"And I second that thank you," Darcy added. "I do need a lady just like Elizabeth to help me through life."

His aunt held out her hand to him, and he took it. "May it be as happy a life as your mother's was." Tears once again glistened in his aunt's eyes as she drew a deep breath. "Now, if you will excuse me, I must find my daughter."

She paused to give Georgiana a hug and express her happiness in having had her join them at Rosings, and then, with determined steps, she headed to the side garden.

Darcy stared after her for a moment. He had not expected her to capitulate so quickly on the idea that she wished for him to be happy even if it was with someone other than Anne.

"Are you ladies ready?" He motioned toward the carriage.

"I am," Georgiana said.

"As am I," Elizabeth agreed. "Sir William and Maria arrived last evening," she said as they moved toward the carriage. "Maria is feeling perfectly well now." That was why the girl had not travelled with Elizabeth as had been planned. "She is sorry, of course, that she will not be here with me as she had hoped, but she is utterly delighted about the reason that I am not staying. My mother and younger sisters have already arrived at my uncle's house in Gracechurch Street." She stood next to the carriage while Darcy helped Georgiana.

"And did you receive word about your aunt and sister Jane?" he asked.

She smiled brightly. "I have had the most wonderful news. My father has always said that the news of one wedding inspires others, and he is correct. Mr. Bingley has offered for Jane. Is that not the most wonderful news?"

"Oh, indeed, it is!" Georgiana cried. "I cannot wait to meet her and your other sisters."

"And I cannot wait to introduce them to you, though I must caution you again that my younger sisters are not as sensible as you are."

"I am not afraid of that. I am certain I can manage. I just survived three weeks of my aunt."

"And my cousin," Elizabeth added with a laugh.

"Yes, I suppose, that, too, though I was not going to say so."

"Of course, you were not. You are all that is polite and genteel." Elizabeth took Darcy's hand, and he lifted her fingers to his lips before assisting her.

"My father sent a letter to you," she said. "I will give it to you in the carriage. Sir William said Papa is quite in his element telling one and all about how his daughter charmed the dour Mr. Darcy."

"I deserve the teasing. I was abominable." And Mr. Bennet had been very gracious in his letter that had granted Darcy permission to marry his daughter. It seemed that Mr. Gardiner had put in a good word about Darcy and how he had brought Mr. Bingley to Gracechurch Street to call on Jane. That, coupled with the grovelling apology and request that had been sent from Darcy to Elizabeth's father had done what they needed to do.

"Do you know where we are?" Darcy asked as he handed Elizabeth into the carriage.

"Rosings?" Richard, who had joined them, replied in a tone that seemed to say Darcy's question was completely absurd.

"Well, yes," Darcy agreed as he took his seat next to his cousin. "But I mean in a more figurative sense."

"In that case," Richard said as he entered the carriage after Darcy, "I would say we are both on the precipice of our own very happy futures."

"Have you secured Anne's hand?" Georgiana asked eagerly.

"Not officially, but I suspect I have it."

"Oh, I am so happy!" Georgiana cried.

"As am I," both Richard and Darcy said at the same time.

"You may want to warn your father that Lady Catherine intends to do some husband searching of her own," Darcy said.

"She wants to do what?" Richard asked.

"She wants to look for a husband now that her duty to Anne is done."

"A husband?"

Darcy nodded. "She has been a widow for many years now, and if you wish to marry Anne and not have her in your home making demands, I say it is to your advantage to help her be successful in her search."

Georgiana giggled as Richard groaned. Darcy merely smiled at his Elizabeth and settled back in his seat to enjoy the journey back to town. For the next several hours he would have the pleasure of listening to the banter around him, joining in where he could, and pondering his good fortune in finding the dividing line between discretion and avarice where both prudence and happily ever after began.

Author's Note:

Spring Soup, mentioned in chapter 4, is a vegetable soup made with brown broth. If you would like to see the recipe you can find it on gutenburg.org in *The Art of Cookery Made Easy and Refined* by John Mollard, Cook (Second Edition, 1802).

If you enjoyed this book, be sure to let others know by leaving a review.
~*~*~
Want to know when other books in this series will be available?
You can always know what's new with my books by subscribing to my mailing list.

leeniebrown.com/subscribe
(There will, of course, be a thank you gift for joining because I think my readers are awesome!)

More Books by Leenie

You can find all of Leenie's books at this link

bit.ly/LeenieBBooks
where you can explore the collections below
~*~

Dash of Darcy and Companions Collection

Marrying Elizabeth Series

Sweet Possibilities and Sweet Extras

Willow Hall Romances

The Choices Series

Darcy Family Holidays

Darcy and... An Austen-Inspired Collection

Teatime Tales (Sweet Austen-inspired Novelettes)

Other Pens

Touches of Austen

Nature's Fury and Delights (Sweet Regency Novelettes)

About the Author

Leenie Brown has always been a girl with an active imagination, which, while growing up, was both an asset, providing many hours of fun as she played out stories, and a liability, when her older sister and aunt would tell her frightening tales. At one time, they had her convinced Dracula lived in the trunk at the end of the bed she slept in when visiting her grandparents!

Although it has been years since she cowered in her bed in her grandparents' basement, she still has an imagination which occasionally runs away with her, and she feeds it now as she did then □ by reading!

Her heroes, when growing up, were authors, and the worlds they painted with words were (and still are) her favourite playgrounds! Now, as an adult, she spends much of her time in the Regency world, playing with the characters from her favourite Jane Austen novels and those of her own creation.

When she is not traipsing down a trail in an attempt to keep up with her imagination, Leenie resides in the beautiful province of Nova Scotia with her two sons and her very own Mr. Brown (a wonderful mix of all the best of Darcy,

Bingley, and Edmund with a healthy dose of the teasing Mr. Tilney and just a dash of the scolding Mr. Knightley).

Connect with Leenie

www.ingramcontent.com/pod-product-compliance
Lightning Source LLC
Chambersburg PA
CBHW072042170626
46811CB00008B/3126